JACK'S TREE

Georgia Byng

Illustrated by Lucy Su

Read all about my battle with the nasty park keeper!

A & C Black • London

For my dad, who loves trees. GB

comix

1 **Joker** · Anthony Masters
2 **Sam's Dream** · Michael Hardcastle
3 **Arf and the Greedy Grabber** · Philip Wooderson
4 **Jack's Tree** · Georgia Byng
5 **The Planet Machine** · Steve Bowkett
6 **Mr Potts the Potty Teacher** · Colin West

First paperback edition 2001
First published 2000 in hardback by
A & C Black (Publishers) Ltd
35 Bedford Row, London WC1R 4JH

Text copyright © 2000 Georgia Byng
Illustrations copyright © 2000 Lucy Su

ISBN 0-7136-5405-8

A CIP catalogue for this book is available from the
British Library.

Printed and bound in Spain by G. Z. Printek, Bilbao

CHAPTER ONE

Jack lived in a jungle. A concrete jungle — the city.

Jack liked his bike and he was good on a skateboard, but what he *loved* was...

... climbing trees.

Maybe Jack had copied this interest from his father, who was a tree surgeon, or maybe he just liked getting away from people and noise.

Whatever the reason, Jack loved the challenge of a tree and...

Although...

... Jack often found that people didn't like him climbing trees.

Mr Fowler was Jack's form teacher. Reluctantly Jack slipped down... down to a telling-off at the bottom.

How **often** have I told you not to climb that tree? Who do you think you are? Tarzan? You're like a filthy monkey the way you climb.

And you're like a scaly old lizard.

Jack watched Mr Fowler's twisted face as he told him off.

And furthermore, I read your work today for the 'Progress and Roads' project. It was **very** silly of you to suggest that pavements in the city should be covered in **grass**. This nonsense has **got** to **stop**. And you have got to **stop climbing trees!**

Mr Fowler had no feeling for nature. He was the sort of person animals would run away from.

Jack set off for home.

Jack walked along the pavement.

He walked through the shopping precinct...

... and across the park. There were very few parks in this part of the city. They were a relief from all the concrete and tarmac. Jack walked to his favourite tree.

In a few moments, Jack was climbing.

Maybe this time he'd get some peace and quiet... at the top, out of reach. But it was not to be.

CHAPTER TWO

It was the park keeper.

Jack suddenly felt very cross. He wasn't hurting anyone by being up the tree.

As he waited below, the park keeper had a very smug look on his face.

Anyway, glad to say, I won't be having to tell you to get down from that tree after tomorrow...

Why? Are you leaving the park?

Jack couldn't help looking hopeful.

Jack looked puzzled.
The park keeper smiled nastily.

To start with, Jack was lost for words.

Then the park keeper grew stern again.

Jack gladly walked away. Inside, he felt mad... really angry about the tree and the fact that the park keeper didn't care.

He talked about getting rid of that tree as if it was a bit of rubbish.

MILLIONS OF TREES LOST FOREVER IN FRENCH STORM

I wish I was a grown-up. Then I'd tell them.

CHAPTER THREE

By the time Jack arrived home he was furious.

Jack's mum and dad were both home.

Jack walked down the hall, past all his dad's tree surgeon gear...

... and into the kitchen.

Jack was not in a light mood.

Have you heard about the tree in Evergreen Park? They're going to chop it down tomorrow. Dad, maybe you know the company that's doing the felling. Can you stop them?

Jack's dad sighed.

Jack couldn't believe it.

But that tree is older than the Houses of Parliament. They wouldn't go and knock **that** down, because of all the important people who've been in it.

There have been protests about that tree, Jack. Remember those people getting signatures outside the supermarket? People tried, but the council didn't listen.

Jack spent the rest of the evening brooding.

It was like waiting for the execution of a friend.

He tried to sleep but he tossed and turned.

At 4 am Jack realised what he should do.

Jack got dressed and took a blanket from his bed.

Then he quietly went to the kitchen and filled a rucksack with food.

He left a note.

Then, loaded up,

he left the house.

He walked quickly through the dark streets,

and hurried to the park gates.

Jack climbed over.

Soon he was beneath the tree. There it stood, silent except for the rustling of its leaves. Jack patted its trunk.

He found himself a comfortable spot, high up in the branches. As dawn broke over the city, Jack listened and looked around him.

Then, as the sun climbed higher in the sky, Jack watched and waited.

At 8 am the park gates opened with a creak. Jack prepared himself for the torrent of nasty words that would come out when the park keeper spotted him.

The park keeper was like a bomb, ready to explode. Jack dreaded lighting the fuse, but he had to do it.

The park keeper's face was growing redder and angrier by the second.

The park keeper was furious. He couldn't climb trees.

Then, to his delight, the tree fellers arrived.

The tree fellers were a mean pair.

The park keeper had called a policeman.
He was aggressive straight away.

Jack could feel that they all hated him. But he didn't
come down. He knew he had to save the tree.

By 9 o'clock, some of the dog-walkers and joggers had
stopped to see what all the commotion was about.

A policewoman arrived.
She tried a softer approach.

The policeman had suddenly had enough.

Right, I'm coming up to get you.

And he began to climb.

Up and up.

But Jack climbed higher too.

He's dangerously high.

He's out of reach.

The lighter branches wouldn't support the policeman's weight.

The policeman was determined.

Half an hour later, a crane was brought under the tree.
A really big crowd was gathering.

The policeman climbed into the crane.
Slowly, menacingly, it moved towards Jack.

Soon, the policeman was only a metre away from Jack.
There was nothing for it.
Jack took a deep breath...

... and jumped like a squirrel on to another branch.

Jack hoped the policeman wouldn't risk that again.

And then Jack saw a fantastic sight.
In the street by the park...

... a television crew was arriving. *This* was what Jack
had hoped would happen.

CHAPTER FOUR

The TV crew chatted to the police and borrowed the crane.

Jack waited, his heart beating fast as they were hoisted up.

A big furry mike dangled over Jack.
His first ever TV interview was about to begin.

Jack argued the tree's case. All over the country that lunch-time people watched and listened to Jack.

His mum was extremely surprised.

And that was how the news spread.

By 2 o'clock the park was really starting to fill.

The police didn't know what to do about this tree boy. Jack's form teacher, Mr Fowler, arrived. He assured the police that he could get Jack down. He was given a megaphone.

Stop all this nonsense and come down now.
You've made your point.
So be grown up about this...
Be **responsible** now...

Watching his teacher's cold face, Jack suddenly lost his temper.

Responsible?

The crowd fell silent.

Is it **responsible** to hack this tree down?

The crowd listened and then...

... they cheered.

During the next hour all sorts of business went on below. The mayor arrived with his councillors. The local Member of Parliament arrived too.

The Mayor and the Member of Parliament continued their hushed conversation.

This will be very bad for my political party. We'll lose votes if people think we don't care about the environment. We'll have to stop the chop!

And so a document was drawn up by a lawyer.

And the Mayor, all the councillors and the local Member of Parliament...

... signed it.

Jack's mum stepped out of the crowd and asked to be taken up in the crane.

Jack trusted his mum, so he gave her the blanket and his bag. Then he climbed down the tree.

But when he got to the bottom, his feet didn't touch the ground.

People lifted him up on to their shoulders and carried him round the tree cheering. Jack was a bit embarrassed.

Then he was carried to the TV crew's van, where he gave one more interview.

Jack was given a warning by the police.

Then Jack's dad arrived.

Jack realised something that day. He wrote it in his diary.

CHAPTER FIVE

After the tree week, everything went back to normal.
Well, nearly. Jack got more letters than before...

And the tree was a bit different too.

THANK
YOU
JACK